'I KNEW HE WAS
IMAGINING A
REALLY LOVELY
GIRL — ALL CURVES,
CURLS, HEART
AND HIDDEN
CLAWS.'

JEAN RHYS
Born 1890, Roseau, Dominica
Died 1979, Exeter, England

'The Day They Burned the Books' and 'Till September
Petronella' were first published in *Tigers Are Better-Looking*
(1968); and 'Rapunzel, Rapunzel' and 'I Used to Live Here
Once' in *Sleep it Off, Lady* (1976). They can all be found in
The Collected Short Stories (2017).

JEAN RHYS

Till September Petronella

PENGUIN BOOKS

PENGUIN CLASSICS

UK | USA | Canada | Ireland | Australia
India | New Zealand | South Africa

Penguin Books is part of the Penguin Random House group
of companies whose addresses can be found at
global.penguinrandomhouse.com.

This selection first published 2018

008

Copyright © 1960, 1962, 1963, 1966, 1967, 1976 by Jean Rhys

The moral rights of the author have been asserted

Set in 10.25/12.75 pt Dante MT Std
Typeset by Jouve (UK), Milton Keynes
Printed in Great Britain by Clays Ltd, Elcograf S.p.A.

ISBN: 978-0-241-33758-5

www.greenpenguin.co.uk

Contents

The Day They Burned the Books

My friend Eddie was a small, thin boy. You could see the blue veins in his wrists and temples. People said that he had consumption and wasn't long for this world. I loved, but sometimes despised him.

His father, Mr Sawyer, was a strange man. Nobody could make out what he was doing in our part of the world at all. He was not a planter or a doctor or a lawyer or a banker. He didn't keep a store. He wasn't a schoolmaster or a government official. He wasn't – that was the point – a gentleman. We had several resident romantics who had fallen in love with the moon on the Caribbees – they were all gentlemen and quite unlike Mr Sawyer who hadn't an 'h' in his composition. Besides, he detested the moon and everything else about the Caribbean and he didn't mind telling you so.

He was agent for a small steamship line which in those days linked up Venezuela and Trinidad with the smaller islands, but he couldn't make much out of that. He must have a private income, people decided, but they never decided why he had chosen to settle in a place he didn't like and to marry a coloured woman. Though a decent, respectable, nicely educated coloured woman, mind you.

Mrs Sawyer must have been very pretty once but, what with one thing and another, that was in days gone by.

When Mr Sawyer was drunk – this often happened – he used to be very rude to her. She never answered him.

'Look at the nigger showing off,' he would say; and she would smile as if she knew she ought to see the joke but couldn't. 'You damned, long-eyed, gloomy half-caste, you don't smell right,' he would say; and she never answered, not even to whisper, 'You don't smell right to me, either.'

The story went that once they had ventured to give a dinner party and that when the servant, Mildred, was bringing in coffee, he had pulled Mrs Sawyer's hair. 'Not a wig, you see,' he bawled. Even then, if you can believe it, Mrs Sawyer had laughed and tried to pretend that it was all part of the joke, this mysterious, obscure, sacred English joke.

But Mildred told the other servants in the town that her eyes had gone wicked, like a soucriant's eyes, and that afterwards she had picked up some of the hair he pulled out and put it in an envelope, and that Mr Sawyer ought to look out (hair is obeah as well as hands).

Of course, Mrs Sawyer had her compensations. They lived in a very pleasant house in Hill Street. The garden was large and they had a fine mango tree, which bore prolifically. The fruit was small, round, very sweet and juicy – a lovely, red-and-yellow colour when it was ripe. Perhaps it was one of the compensations, I used to think.

Mr Sawyer built a room on to the back of this house. It was unpainted inside and the wood smelt very sweet. Bookshelves lined the walls. Every time the Royal Mail steamer came in it brought a package for him, and gradually the empty shelves filled.

Once I went there with Eddie to borrow *The Arabian Nights*. That was on a Saturday afternoon, one of those hot, still afternoons when you felt that everything had gone to sleep, even the water in the gutters. But Mrs Sawyer was not asleep. She put her head in at the door and looked at us, and I knew that she hated the room and hated the books.

It was Eddie with the pale blue eyes and straw-coloured hair – the living image of his father, though often as silent as his mother – who first infected me with doubts about 'home', meaning England. He would be so quiet when others who had never seen it – none of us had ever seen it – were talking about its delights, gesticulating freely as we talked – London, the beautiful, rosy-cheeked ladies, the theatres, the shops, the fog, the blazing coal fires in winter, the exotic food (whitebait eaten to the sound of violins), strawberries and cream – the word 'strawberries' always spoken with a guttural and throaty sound which we imagined to be the proper English pronunciation.

'I don't like strawberries,' Eddie said on one occasion.

'You *don't like* strawberries?'

'No, and I don't like daffodils either. Dad's always going on about them. He says they lick the flowers here into a cocked hat and I bet that's a lie.'

We were all too shocked to say, 'You don't know a thing about it.' We were so shocked that nobody spoke to him for

3

the rest of the day. But I for one admired him. I also was tired of learning and reciting poems in praise of daffodils, and my relations with the few 'real' English boys and girls I had met were awkward. I had discovered that if I called myself English they would snub me haughtily: 'You're not English; you're a horrid colonial.' 'Well, I don't much want to be English,' I would say. 'It's much more fun to be French or Spanish or something like that – and, as a matter of fact, I am a bit.' Then I was too killingly funny, quite ridiculous. Not only a horrid colonial, but also ridiculous. Heads I win, tails you lose – that was the English. I had thought about all this, and thought hard, but I had never dared to tell anybody what I thought and I realized that Eddie had been very bold.

But he was bold, and stronger than you would think. For one thing, he never felt the heat; some coldness in his fair skin resisted it. He didn't burn red or brown, he didn't freckle much.

Hot days seemed to make him feel especially energetic. 'Now we'll run twice round the lawn and then you can pretend you're dying of thirst in the desert and that I'm an Arab chieftain bringing you water.

'You must drink slowly,' he would say, 'for if you're very thirsty and you drink quickly you die.'

So I learnt the voluptuousness of drinking slowly when you are very thirsty – small mouthful by small mouthful, until the glass of pink, iced Coca-Cola was empty.

Just after my twelfth birthday Mr Sawyer died suddenly, and as Eddie's special friend I went to the funeral, wearing a new white dress. My straight hair was damped with sugar and water the night before and plaited into tight little plaits, so that it should be fluffy for the occasion.

When it was all over everybody said how nice Mrs Sawyer had looked, walking like a queen behind the coffin and crying her eyeballs out at the right moment, and wasn't Eddie a funny boy? He hadn't cried at all.

After this Eddie and I took possession of the room with the books. No one else ever entered it, except Mildred to sweep and dust in the mornings, and gradually the ghost of Mr Sawyer pulling Mrs Sawyer's hair faded, though this took a little time. The blinds were always halfway down and going in out of the sun was like stepping into a pool of brown-green water. It was empty except for the bookshelves, a desk with a green baize top and a wicker rocking-chair.

'My room,' Eddie called it. 'My books,' he would say, 'my books.'

I don't know how long this lasted. I don't know whether it was weeks after Mr Sawyer's death or months after, that I see myself and Eddie in the room. But there we are and there, unexpectedly, are Mrs Sawyer and Mildred. Mrs Sawyer's mouth tight, her eyes pleased. She is pulling all the books out of the shelves and piling them into two heaps. The big, fat glossy ones – the good-looking ones, Mildred explains in a whisper – lie in one heap. The *Encyclopaedia Britannica*, *British Flowers*, *Birds and Beasts*, various histories, books with maps, Froude's *English in the West Indies* and so on – they are going to be sold. The unimportant books, with paper covers or damaged covers or torn pages, lie in another heap. They are going to be burnt – yes, burnt.

Mildred's expression was extraordinary as she said that – half hugely delighted, half shocked, even frightened. And as for Mrs Sawyer – well, I knew bad temper (I had often seen it), I knew rage, but this was hate. I recognized the difference at once and stared at her curiously. I edged closer to her so that I could see the titles of the books she was handling.

It was the poetry shelf. *Poems*, Lord Byron, *Poetical Works*, Milton, and so on. Vlung, vlung, vlung – all thrown into the heap that were to be sold. But a book by Christina Rossetti, though also bound in leather, went into the heap that was to be burnt, and by a flicker in Mrs Sawyer's eyes I knew that worse than men who wrote books were women who wrote books – infinitely worse. Men could be mercifully shot; women must be tortured.

Mrs Sawyer did not seem to notice that we were there, but she was breathing free and easy and her hands had got the rhythm of tearing and pitching. She looked beautiful, too – beautiful as the sky outside which was a very dark blue, or the mango tree, long sprays of brown and gold.

When Eddie said 'no', she did not even glance at him.

'No,' he said again in a high voice. 'Not that one. I was reading that one.'

She laughed and he rushed at her, his eyes starting out of his head, shrieking, 'Now I've got to hate you too. Now I hate you too.'

He snatched the book out of her hand and gave her a violent push. She fell into the rocking-chair.

Well, I wasn't going to be left out of all this, so I grabbed a book from the condemned pile and dived under Mildred's outstretched arm.

Then we were both in the garden. We ran along the path, bordered with crotons. We pelted down the path though they did not follow us and we could hear Mildred laughing – kyah, kyah, kyah, kyah. As I ran I put the book I had taken into the loose front of my brown holland dress. It felt warm and alive.

When we got into the street we walked sedately, for we feared the black children's ridicule. I felt very happy, because I had saved this book and it was my book and I would read it from the beginning to the triumphant words 'The End'. But I was uneasy when I thought of Mrs Sawyer.

'What will she do?' I said.

'Nothing,' Eddie said. 'Not to me.'

He was white as a ghost in his sailor suit, a blue-white even in the setting sun, and his father's sneer was clamped on his face.

'But she'll tell your mother all sorts of lies about you,' he said. 'She's an awful liar. She can't make up a story to save her life, but she makes up lies about people all right.'

'My mother won't take any notice of her,' I said. Though I was not at all sure.

'Why not? Because she's . . . because she isn't white?'

Well, I knew the answer to that one. Whenever the subject

was brought up – people's relations and whether they had a drop of coloured blood or whether they hadn't – my father would grow impatient and interrupt. 'Who's white?' he would say. 'Damned few.'

So I said, 'Who's white? Damned few.'

'You can go to the devil,' Eddie said. 'She's prettier than your mother. When she's asleep her mouth smiles and she has your curling eyelashes and quantities and quantities and *quantities* of hair.'

'Yes,' I said truthfully. 'She's prettier than my mother.'

It was a red sunset that evening, a huge, sad, frightening sunset.

'Look, let's go back,' I said. 'If you're sure she won't be vexed with you, let's go back. It'll be dark soon.'

At his gate he asked me not to go. 'Don't go yet, don't go yet.'

We sat under the mango tree and I was holding his hand when he began to cry. Drops fell on my hand like the water from the dripstone in the filter in our yard. Then I began to cry too and when I felt my own tears on my hand I thought, 'Now perhaps we're married.

'Yes, certainly, now we're married,' I thought. But I didn't say anything. I didn't say a thing until I was sure he had stopped. Then I asked, 'What's your book?'

'It's *Kim*,' he said. 'But it got torn. It starts at page twenty now. What's the one you took?'

'I don't know, it's too dark to see,' I said.

When I got home I rushed into my bedroom and locked

the door because I knew that this book was the most important thing that had ever happened to me and I did not want anybody to be there when I looked at it.

But I was very disappointed, because it was in French and seemed dull. *Fort Comme La Mort*, it was called . . .

Till September Petronella

There was a barrel organ playing at the corner of Torrington Square. It played 'Destiny' and 'La Palome' and 'Le Rêve Passe', all tunes I liked, and the wind was warm and kind not spiteful, which doesn't often happen in London. I packed the striped dress that Estelle had helped me to choose, and the cheap white one that fitted well, and my best underclothes, feeling very happy while I was packing. A bit of a change, for that had not been one of my lucky summers.

I would tell myself it was the colour of the carpet or something about my room which was depressing me, but it wasn't that. And it wasn't anything to do with money either. I was making nearly five pounds a week – very good for me, and different from when I first started, when I was walking round trying to get work. *No* Hawkers, *No* Models, some of them put up, and you stand there, your hands cold and clammy, afraid to ring the bell. But I had got past that state; this depression had nothing to do with money.

I often wished I was like Estelle, this French girl who lived in the big room on the ground floor. She had everything so cut-and-dried, she walked the tightrope so beautifully, not even knowing she was walking it. I'd think about the talks we had, and her clothes and her scent and the way she did her hair, and that when I went into her room it didn't seem like a Bloomsbury bed-sitting room – and when it comes to Bloomsbury bed-sitting rooms I know what I'm talking about. No, it was like a room out of one of those long, romantic novels, six hundred and fifty pages of small print, translated from French or German or Hungarian or something – because few of the English ones have the exact feeling I mean. And you read one page of it or even one phrase of it, and then you gobble up all the rest and go about in a dream for weeks afterwards, for months afterwards – perhaps all your life, who knows? – surrounded by those six hundred and fifty pages, the houses, the streets, the snow, the river, the roses, the girls, the sun, the ladies' dresses and the gentlemen's voices, the old, wicked, hard-hearted women and the old, sad women, the waltz music, everything. What is not there you put in afterwards, for it is alive, this book, and it grows in your head. 'The house I was living in when I read that book,' you think, or 'This colour reminds me of that book.'

It was after Estelle left, telling me she was going to Paris and wasn't sure whether she was coming back, that I struck a bad patch. Several of the people I was sitting to left London in June, but, instead of arranging for more work, I took long walks, zigzag, always the same way – Euston Road, Hampstead Road, Camden Town – though I hated those streets, which were like a grey nightmare in the sun. You saw so many old women, or women who seemed old, peering at the vegetables in the Camden Town market, looking at you with hatred, or blankly, as though they had forgotten your language, and talked another one. 'My God,' I would think, 'I hope I never live to be old. Anyway, however old I get, I'll never let my hair go grey. I'll dye it black, red, any colour you like, but I'll never let it go grey. I hate grey too much.' Coming back from one of these walks the thought came to me suddenly, like a revelation, that I could kill myself any time I liked and so end it. After that I put a better face on things.

When Marston wrote and I told the landlord I was going away for a fortnight, he said 'So there's a good time coming for the ladies, is there? – a good time coming for the girls? About time too.'

Marston said, 'You seem very perky, my dear. I hardly recognized you.'

I looked along the platform, but Julian had not come to meet me. There was only Marston, his long, white face and his pale-blue eyes, smiling.

'What a gigantic suitcase,' he said. 'I have my motorbike here, but I suppose I'd better leave it. We'll take a cab.'

It was getting dark when we reached the cottage, which stood by itself on rising ground. There were two elm trees in a field near the veranda, but the country looked bare, with low, grassy hills.

As we walked up the path through the garden I could hear Julian laughing and a girl talking, her voice very high and excited, though she put on a calm, haughty expression as we came into the room. Her dress was red, and she wore several coloured glass bangles which tinkled when she moved.

Marston said, 'This is Frankie. You've met the great Julian, of course.'

Well, I knew Frankie Morell by sight, but as she didn't say anything about it I didn't either. We smiled at each other cautiously, falsely.

The table was laid for four people. The room looked comfortable but there were no flowers. I had expected that they would have it full of flowers. However, there were some sprays of honeysuckle in a green jug in my bedroom and Marston, standing in the doorway, said, 'I walked miles to get you that honeysuckle this morning. I thought about you all the time I was picking it.'

'Don't be long,' he said. 'We're all very hungry.'

We ate ham and salad and drank perry. It went to my head a bit. Julian talked about his job which he seemed to dislike. He was the music critic of one of the daily papers. 'It's a scandal. One's forced to down the right people and praise the wrong people.'

'Forced?' said Marston.

'Well, they drop very strong hints.'

'I'll take the plates away,' Frankie told me. 'You can start tomorrow. Not one of the local women will do a thing for us. We've only been here a fortnight, but they've got up a hate you wouldn't believe. Julian says he almost faints when he thinks of it. I say, why think of it?'

When she came back she turned the lamp out. Down there it was very still. The two trees outside did not move, or the moon.

Julian lay on the sofa and I was looking at his face and his hair when Marston put his arms round me and kissed me. But I watched Julian and listened to him whistling – stopping, laughing, beginning again.

'What was that music?' I said, and Frankie answered in a patronizing voice, '*Tristan*, second act duet.'

'I've never been to that opera.'

I had never been to any opera. All the same, I could imagine it. I could imagine myself in a box, wearing a moonlight-blue dress and silver shoes, and when the lights went up everybody asking, 'Who's that lovely girl in that box?' But it must happen quickly or it will be too late.

Marston squeezed my hand. 'Very fine performance, Julian,' he said, 'very fine. Now forgive me, my dears, I must leave you. All this emotion –'

Julian lighted the lamp, took a book from the shelf and began to read.

Frankie blew on the nails of one hand and polished them on the edge of the other. Her nails were nice – of course, you could get a manicure for a bob then – but her hands were large and too white for her face. 'I've seen you at the Apple Tree, surely.' The Apple Tree was a nightclub in Greek Street.

'Oh yes, often.'

'But you've cut your hair. I wanted to cut mine, but Julian asked me not to. He begged me not to. Didn't you, Julian?'

Julian did not answer.

'He said he'd lose his strength if I cut my hair.'

Julian turned over a page and went on reading.

'This is not a bad spot, is it?' Frankie said. 'Not one of those places where the ceiling's on top of your head and you've got to walk four miles in the dark to the lavatory. There are two other bedrooms besides the one Marston gave you. Come and have a look at them. You can change over if you want to. We'll never tear Julian away from his book. It's about the biological inferiority of women. That's what you told me, Julian, isn't it?'

'Oh, *go* away,' Julian said.

We ended up in her room, where she produced some head and figure studies, photographs.

'Do you like these? Do you know this man? He says I'm the best model he's ever had. He says I'm far and away the best model in London.'

'Beautiful. Lovely photographs.'

But Frankie, sitting on the big bed, said, 'Aren't people swine? Julian says I never think. He's wrong, sometimes I think quite a lot. The other day I spent a long time trying to decide which were worse – men or women.'

'I wonder.'

'Women are worse.'

She had long, calm black hair, drawn away from her face and hanging smoothly almost to her waist, and a calm, clear little voice and a calm, haughty expression.

'They'll kick your face to bits if you let them. And shriek with laughter at the damage. But I'm not going to let them – oh no . . . Marston's always talking about you,' she said. 'He's very fond of you, poor old Marston. Do you know that picture as you go into his studio – in the entrance place? What's he say it is?'

'The Apotheosis of Lust.'

'Yes, the Apotheosis of Lust. I have to laugh when I think of that, for some reason. Poor old Andy Marston . . . But I don't know why I should say "Poor old Andy Marston". He'll always have one penny to tinkle against another. His family's very wealthy, you know.'

'He makes me go cold.'

I thought, 'Why did I say that?' Because I like Marston.

'So that's how you feel about him, is it?' She seemed pleased, as if she had heard something she wanted to hear, had been waiting to hear.

'Are you tired?' Marston said.

I was looking out of the bedroom window at some sheep feeding in the field where the elm trees grew.

'A bit,' I said. 'A bit very.'

His mouth drooped, disappointed.

'Oh, Marston, thank you for asking me down here. It's lovely to get away from London; it's like a dream.'

'A dream, my God! However, when it comes to dreams, why shouldn't they be pleasant?'

He sat down on the windowsill.

'The great Julian's not so bad, is he?'

'Why do you call him the great Julian? As if you were gibing at him.'

'Gibing at him? Good Lord, far be it from me to gibe at him. He *is* the great Julian. He's going to be very important, so far as an English musician can be important. He's horribly conceited, though. Not about his music, of course – he's conceited about his personal charm. I can't think why. He's a very ordinary type really. You see that nose and mouth and hear that voice all over the place. You rather dislike him, don't you?'

'Do I?'

'Of course you do. Have you forgotten how annoyed you were when I told you that he'd have to *see* a female before he could consent to live at close quarters with her for two weeks? You were quite spirited about it, I thought. Don't say that was only a flash in the pan, you poor devil of a female, female, female, in a country where females are only tolerated at best! What's going to become of you, Miss Petronella Gray, living in a bed-sitting room in Torrington Square, with no money, no background and no nous? . . . Is Petronella your real name?'

'Yes.'

'You worry me, whatever your name is. I bet it isn't Gray.'

I thought, 'What does it matter? If you knew how bloody my home was you wouldn't be surprised that I wanted to change my name and forget all about it.'

I said, not looking at him, 'I was called after my grandmother – Julia Petronella.'

'Oh, you've got a grandmother, have you? Fancy that! Now, for Heaven's sake don't put on that expression. Take my advice and grow another skin or two and sharpen your claws before it's too late. *Before it's too late*, mark those words. If you don't, you're going to have a hell of a time.'

'So that I long for death?'

He looked startled. 'Why do you say that?'

'It was only the first thing that came into my head from nowhere. I was joking.'

When he did not answer, 'Well, goodnight,' I said. 'Sleep tight.'

'I shan't sleep,' he said. 'I shall probably have to listen to those two for quite a time yet. When they're amorous they're noisy and when they fight it's worse. She goes for him with a penknife. Mind you, she only does that because he likes it, but her good nature is a pretence. She's a bitch really. Shut your door and you won't hear anything. Will you be sad tomorrow?'

'Of course not.'

'Don't look as if you'd lost a shilling and found a sixpence then,' he said, and went out.

That's the way they always talk. 'You look as if you'd lost a shilling and found sixpence,' they say; 'You look very perky, I hardly recognized you,' they say; *'Look gay,'* they say. 'My dear Petronella, I have an entirely new idea of you. I'm going to paint you out in the opulent square. So can you wear something gay tomorrow afternoon? Not one of those drab affairs you usually clothe yourself in. Gay – do you know the meaning of the word? Think about it, it's very important.'

The things you remember . . .

Once, left alone in a very ornate studio, I went up to a plaster cast – the head of a man, one of those Greek heads – and kissed it, because it was so beautiful. Its mouth felt warm, not cold. It was smiling. When I kissed it the room went dead silent and I was frightened. I told Estelle about this one day. 'Does that sound mad?' She didn't laugh. She said, 'Who hasn't kissed a picture or a photograph and suddenly been frightened?'

The music Julian had been whistling was tormenting me. That, and the blind eyes of the plaster cast, and the way the sun shone on the black iron bedstead in my room in Torrington Square on fine days. The bars of the bedstead grin at me. Sometimes I count the knobs on the chest of drawers three times over. 'One of those drab affairs! . . .'

I began to talk to Julian in my head. Was it to Julian? 'I'm not like that. I'm not at all like that. They're trying to make me like that, but I'm not like that.'

After a while I took a pencil and paper and wrote, 'I love Julian. Julian, I kissed you once, but you didn't know.'

I folded the paper several times and hid it under some clothes in my suitcase. Then I went to bed and slept at once.

Where our path joined the main road there were some cottages. As Marston and I came back from our walk next morning we passed two women in their gardens, which were full of lupins and poppies. They looked at us sullenly, as though they disliked us. When Marston said 'Good morning', they did not answer.

'Surly, priggish brutes,' he muttered, 'but that's how they are.'

The grass round our cottage was long and trampled in places. There were no flowers.

'They're back,' Marston said. 'There's the motorbike.'

They came out on to the veranda, very spruce; Frankie in her red frock with her hair tied up in a red and blue handkerchief, Julian wearing a brown coat over a blue shirt and shabby grey trousers like Marston's. Very gay, I thought. (*Gay – do you know the meaning of the word?*)

'What's the matter with you, Marston?' Julian said. 'You look frightful.'

'You do seem a bit upset,' Frankie said. 'What happened? Do tell.'

'Don't tell her anything,' said Marston. 'I'm going to dress up too. Why should I be the only one in this resplendent assembly with a torn shirt and stained bags? Wait till you see what I've got – and I don't mean what you mean.'

'Let's get the food ready,' Frankie said to me.

The kitchen table was covered with things they had brought from Cheltenham, and there were several bottles of white wine cooling in a bucket of water in the corner.

'What have you done to Marston?'

'Nothing. What on earth do you mean?'

Nothing had happened. We were sitting under a tree, looking at a field of corn, and Marston put his head in my lap and then a man came along and yelled at us. I said, 'What do you think we're doing to your corn? Can't we even look at your corn?' But Marston only mumbled, 'I'm fearfully sorry. I'm dreadfully sorry', and so on. And then we went walking along the main road in the sun, not talking much because I was hating him.

'Nothing happened,' I said.

'Oh well, it's a pity, because Julian's in a bad mood today. However, don't take any notice of him. Don't start a row whatever you do, just smooth it over.'

'Look at the lovely bit of steak I got,' she said. 'Marston says he can't touch any meat except cold ham, I ask you, and he does the cooling. Cold ham and risotto, risotto and cold ham. And curried eggs. That's what we've been living on ever since we came down here.'

When we went in with the food they had finished a bottle of wine. Julian said, 'Here's luck to the ruddy citizens I saw this morning. May they be flourishing and producing offspring exactly like themselves, but far, far worse, long after we are all in our dishonoured graves.'

Marston was now wearing black silk pyjamas with a pattern of red and green dragons. His long, thin neck and sad face looked extraordinary above this get-up. Frankie and I glanced at each other and giggled. Julian scowled at me.

Marston went over to the mirror. 'Never mind,' he said softly to his reflection, 'never mind, never mind.'

'It's ham and salad again,' Frankie said. 'But I've got some prunes.'

The table was near the window. A hot, white glare shone in our eyes. We tried pulling the blinds down, but one got stuck and we went on eating in the glare.

Then Frankie talked about the steak again. 'You must have your first bite tonight, Marston.'

'It won't be my first bite,' Marston said. 'I've been persuaded to taste beef before.'

'Oh, you never told me that. No likee?'

'I thought it would taste like sweat,' Marston said, 'and it did.'

Frankie looked annoyed. 'The trouble with you people is that you try to put other people off just because you don't fancy a thing. If you'd just not like it and leave it at that, but you don't *rest* till you've put everybody else off.'

'Oh God, let's get tight,' Julian said. 'There are bottles and bottles of wine in the kitchen. Cooling, I hope.'

'We'll get them,' Frankie said, 'we'll get them.'

Frankie sat on the kitchen table. 'I think Julian's spoiling for a fight. Let him calm down a bit . . . you're staving Marston off, aren't you? And he doesn't like it; he's very disconsolate. You've got to be careful of these people, they can be as hard as nails.'

Far away a dog barked, a cock crew, somebody was sawing wood. I hardly noticed what she had said because again it came, that feeling of happiness, the fish-in-water feeling, so that I couldn't even remember having been unhappy.

Frankie started on a long story about a man called Petersen who had written a play about Northern gods and goddesses and Yggdrasil.

'I thought Yggdrasil was a girl, but it seems it's a tree.'

Marston and Julian and all that lot had taken Petersen up,

she said. They used to ask him out and make him drunk. Then he would take his clothes off and dance about and if he did not do it somebody would be sure to say, 'What's the matter? Why don't you perform?' But as soon as he got really sordid they had dropped him like a hot brick. He simply disappeared.

'I met an old boy who knew him and asked what had happened. The old boy said, "A gigantic maw has swallowed Petersen . . ." Maw, what a word! It reminds me of Julian's mother – she's a maw if you like. Well, I'd better take these bottles along now.'

So we took the four bottles out of the bucket and went back into the sitting-room. It was still hot and glaring, but not quite so bad as it had been.

'Now it's my turn to make a speech,' said Marston. 'But you must drink, pretty creatures, drink.' He filled our glasses and I drank mine quickly. He filled it up again.

'My speech,' he said, 'my speech . . . Let's drink to afternoon, the best of all times. Cruel morning is past, fearful, unpredictable, lonely night is yet to come. Here's to heartrending afternoon . . . I will now recite a poem. It's hackneyed and pawed about, like so many other things, but beautiful. *"C'est bien la pire peine de ne savoir pourquoi –"'*

He stopped and began to cry. We all looked at him. Nobody laughed; nobody knew what to say. I felt shut in by the glare.

Marston blew his nose, wiped his eyes and gabbled on: '*"Pourquoi, sans amour et sans haine, Mon coeur a tant de peine . . ."'*

23

' "*Sans amour*" is right,' Julian said, staring at me. I looked back into his eyes.

' "But for loving, why, you would not, Sweet," ' Marston went on, ' "Though we prayed you, Paid you, brayed you. In a mortar – for you could not, Sweet." '

'The motorbike was altogether a bit of luck,' Frankie said. 'Julian had a fight with a man on the bus going in. I thought he'd have a fit.'

'Fight?' Julian said. 'I never fight. I'm frightened.'

He was still staring at me.

'Well then, you were very rude.'

'I'm never rude, either,' Julian said. 'I'm far too frightened ever to be rude! I suffer in silence.'

'I shouldn't do that if I were you,' I said. The wine was making me giddy. So was the glare, and the way he was looking at me.

'What's this young creature up to?' he said. 'I can't quite make her out.'

'Ruddy respectable citizens never can.'

'Ha-hah,' Frankie said. 'One in the eye for you, Julian. You're always going on about respectable people, but you know *you* are respectable, whatever you say and whatever you do and you'll be respectable till you die, however you die, and that way you miss something, believe it or not.'

'You keep out of this, Phoenician,' Julian said. 'You've got nothing to say. Retire under the table, because that's where I like you best.'

Frankie crawled under the table. She darted her head out

now and again, pretending to bite his legs, and every time she did that he would shiver and scream.

'Oh, come on out,' he said at last. 'It's too hot for these antics.'

Frankie crawled out again, very pleased with herself, went to the mirror and arranged the handkerchief round her hair. 'Am I really like a Phoenician?'

'Of course you are. A Phoenician from Cornwall, England. Direct descent, I should say.'

'And what's she?' Frankie said. Her eyes looked quite different, like snake's eyes. We all looked quite different – it's funny what drink does.

'That's very obvious too,' Julian said.

'All right, why don't you come straight out with it?' I said. 'Or are you frightened?'

'Sometimes words fail.'

Marston waved his arms about. 'Julian, you stop this. I won't have it.'

'You fool,' Julian said, 'you fool. Can't you see she's fifth rate. Can't you see?

'You ghastly cross between a barmaid and a chorus girl,' he said. 'You female spider,' he said. 'You've been laughing at him for weeks,' he said, 'jeering at him, sniggering at him. Stopping him from working – the best painter in this damnable island, the only one in my opinion. And then I try to get him away from you, of course you follow him down here.'

'That's not it at all,' Marston said. 'You're not being fair to the girl. You don't understand her a bit.'

'She doesn't care,' Julian said. 'Look at her – she's giggling her stupid head off.'

'Well, what are you to do when you come up against a mutual admiration society?' I said.

'You're letting your jealousy run away with you,' said Marston.

'Jealousy?' Julian said. 'Jealousy!' He was unrecognizable. His beautiful eyes were little, mean pits and you looked down them into nothingness.

'Jealous of what?' he shrieked. 'Why, do you know that she told Frankie last night that she can't bear you and that the only reason she has anything to do with you is because she wants money. What do you think of that? Does that open your eyes?'

'Now, *Julian*!' Frankie's voice was as loud and high as his. 'You'd no right to repeat that. You promised you wouldn't and anyway you've exaggerated it. It's all very well for you to talk about how inferior women are, but you get more like your horrible mother every moment.'

'You do,' Marston said, quite calm now. 'Julian, you really do.'

'Do you know what all this is about?' Frankie said, nodding at Julian. 'It's because he doesn't want me to go back to London with him. He wants me to go and be patronized and educated by his detestable mother in her dreary house in the dreary country, who will then say that the case is hopeless. Wasn't she a good sort and a saint to try? But the girl is *quite impossible*. Do you think I don't know that trick? It's as old as the hills.

'You're mean,' she said to Julian, 'and you hate girls really. Don't imagine I don't see through you. You're trying to get me down. But you won't do it. If you think you're the only man in the world who's fond of me *or* that I'm a goddamned fool, you're making the hell of a big mistake, you and your mother.'

She plucked a hairpin from her hair, bent it into the shape of pince-nez and went on in a mincing voice, 'Do Ay understend you tew say thet *may* sonn –' she placed the pince-nez on her nose and looked over it sourly '– with *one* connection –'

'Damn you,' said Julian, 'damn you, damn you.'

'Now they're off,' Marston said placidly. 'Drinking on a hot afternoon is a mistake. The penknife will be out in a minute . . . Don't go. Stay and watch the fun. My money on Frankie every time.'

But I went into the bedroom and shut the door. I could hear them wrangling and Marston, very calm and superior, putting in a word now and again. Then nothing. They had gone on to the veranda.

I got the letter I had written and tore it very carefully into four pieces. I spat on each piece. I opened the door – there was not a sign of them. I took the pieces of paper to the lavatory, emptied them in and pulled the plug. As soon as I heard the water gushing I felt better.

The door of the kitchen was open and I saw that there was another path leading to the main road.

And there I was, walking along, not thinking of anything, my eyes fixed on the ground. I walked a long way like that, not looking up, though I passed several people. At last I came to a signpost. I was on the Cirencester road. Something about the word 'miles' written made me feel very tired.

A little farther on the wall on one side of the road was low. It was the same wall on which Marston and I had sat that morning, and he had said, 'Do you think we could rest here or will the very stones rise up against us?' I looked round and there was nobody in sight, so I stepped over it and sat down in the shade. It was pretty country, but bare. The white, glaring look was still in the sky.

Close by there was a dove cooing. 'Coo away, dove,' I thought. 'It's no use, no use, still coo away, coo away.'

After a while the dazed feeling, as if somebody had hit me on the head, began to go. I thought 'Cirencester – and then a train to London. It's as easy as that.'

Then I realized that I had left my handbag and money, as well as everything else, in the bedroom at the cottage, but imagining walking back there made me feel so tired that I could hardly put one foot in front of the other.

I got over the wall. A car that was coming along slowed down and stopped and the man driving it said, 'Want a lift?'

I went up to the car.

'Where do you want to go?'

'I want to go to London.'

'To London? Well, I can't take you as far as that, but I can get you into Cirencester to catch a train if you like.'

I said anxiously, 'Yes – but I must go back first to the place where I've been staying. It's not far.'

'Haven't time for that. I've got an appointment. I'm late already and I mustn't miss it. Tell you what – come along with me. If you'll wait till I've done I can take you to fetch your things.'

I got into the car. As soon as I touched him I felt comforted. Some men are like that.

'Well, you look as if you'd lost a shilling and found sixpence.'

Again I had to laugh.

'That's better. Never does any good to be down in the mouth.

'We're nearly in Cirencester now,' he said after a while. 'I've got to see a lot of people. This is market day and I'm a farmer. I'll take you to a nice quiet place where you can have a cup of tea while you're waiting.'

He drove to a pub in a narrow street. 'This way in.' I followed him into the bar.

'Good afternoon, Mrs Strickland. Lovely day, isn't it? Will you give my friend a cup of tea while I'm away, and make her comfortable? She's very tired.'

'I will, certainly,' Mrs Strickland said, with a swift glance up and down. 'I expect the young lady would like a nice wash too, wouldn't she?' She was dark and nicely got up, but her voice had a tinny sound.

'Oh, I would.'

I looked down at my crumpled white dress. I touched my face for I knew there must be a red mark where I had lain with it pressed against the ground.

'See you later,' the farmer said.

There were brightly polished taps in the ladies' room and a very clean red and black tiled floor. I washed my hands, tried to smooth my dress, and powdered my face – *Poudre Nildé basané* – but I did it without looking in the glass.

Tea and cakes were laid in a small, dark, stuffy room. There were three pictures of Lady Hamilton, Johnny Walker advertisements, china bulldogs wearing sailor caps and two calendars. One said January 9th, but the other was right – July 28th, 1914.

'Well, here I am!' He sat heavily down beside me. 'Did Mrs Strickland look after you all right?'

'Very well.'

'Oh, she's a good sort, she's a nice woman. She's known me a long time. Of course, you haven't, have you? But everything's got to have a start.'

Then he said he hadn't done so badly that afternoon and stretched out his legs, looking pleased, looking happy as the day is long.

'What were you thinking about when I came in? You nearly jumped out of your skin.'

'I was thinking about the time.'

'About the time? Oh, don't worry about that. There's plenty of time.'

He produced a large silver case, took out a cigar and lighted it, long and slow. 'Plenty of time,' he said. 'Dark in here, isn't it? So you live in London, do you?'

'Yes.'

'I've often thought I'd like to know a nice girl up in London.'

His eyes were fixed on Lady Hamilton and I knew he was imagining a really lovely girl – all curves, curls, heart and hidden claws. He swallowed, then put his hand over mine.

'I'd like to feel that when I go up to Town there's a friend I could see and have a good time with. You know. And I could give her a good time too. By God, I could. I know what women like.'

'You do?'

'Yes, I do. They like a bit of loving, that's what they like, isn't it? A bit of loving. All women like that. They like it dressed up sometimes – and sometimes not, it all depends. You have to know, and I know. I just know.'

'You've nothing more to learn, have you?'

'Not in that way I haven't. And they like pretty dresses and bottles of scent, and bracelets with blue stones in them. I know. Well, what about it?' he said, but as if he were joking.

I looked away from him at the calendar and did not answer, making my face blank.

'What about it?' he repeated.

'It's nice of you to say you want to see me again – very polite.'

He laughed. 'You think I'm being polite, do you? Well, perhaps – perhaps not. No harm in asking, was there? No offence meant – or taken, I hope. It's all right. I'll take you to get your things and catch your train – and we'll have a bottle of something good before we start off. It won't hurt you. It's

31

bad stuff hurts you, not good stuff. You haven't found that out yet, but you will. Mrs Strickland has some good stuff, I can tell you – good enough for me, and I want the best.'

So we had a bottle of Clicquot in the bar.

He said, 'It puts some life into you, doesn't it?'

It did too. I wasn't feeling tired when we left the pub, nor even sad.

'Well,' he said as we got into the car, 'you've got to tell me where to drive to. And you don't happen to know a little song, do you?'

'That was very pretty,' he said when I stopped. 'You've got a very pretty voice indeed. Give us some more.'

But we were getting near the cottage and I didn't finish the next song because I was nervous and worried that I wouldn't be able to tell him the right turning.

At the foot of the path I thought, 'The champagne worked all right.'

He got out of the car and came with me. When we reached the gate leading into the garden he stood by my side without speaking.

They were on the veranda. We could hear their voices clearly.

'Listen, fool,' Julian was saying, 'listen, half-wit. What I said yesterday has nothing to do with what I say today or what I shall say tomorrow. Why should it?'

'That's what you think,' Frankie said obstinately. 'I don't agree with you. It might have something to do with it whether you like it or not.'

'Oh, stop arguing, you two,' Marston said. 'It's all very well for you, Julian, but I'm worried about that girl. I'm responsible. She looked so damned miserable. Supposing she's gone and made away with herself. I shall feel awful. Besides, probably I shall be held up to every kind of scorn and obloquy – as usual. And though it's all your fault you'll escape scot-free – also as usual.'

'Are those your friends?' the farmer asked.

'Well, they're my friends in a way . . . I have to go in to get my things. It won't take long.'

Julian said, 'I think, I rather think, Marston, that I hear a female pipe down there. You can lay your fears away. She's not the sort to kill herself. I told you that.'

'Who's that?' the farmer said.

'That's Mr Oakes, one of my hosts.'

'Oh, is it? I don't like the sound of him. I don't like the sound of any of them. Shall I come with you?'

'No, don't. I won't be long.'

I went round by the kitchen into my room, walking very softly. I changed into my dark dress and then began to throw my things into the suitcase. I did all this as quickly as I could, but before I had finished Marston came in, still wearing his black pyjamas crawling with dragons.

'Who were you talking to outside?'

'Oh, that's a man I met. He's going to drive me to Cirencester to catch the London train.'

'You're not offended, are you?'

'Not a bit. Why should I be?'

'Of course, the great Julian can be so difficult,' he murmured. 'But don't think I didn't stick up for you, because I did. I said to him, "It's all very well for you to be rude to a girl I bring down, but what about your loathly Frankie, whom you inflict upon me day after day and week after week and I never say a word? I'm never even sharp to her –" What are you smiling at?'

'The idea of your being sharp to Frankie.'

'The horrid little creature!' Marston said excitedly, 'the unspeakable bitch! But the day will come when Julian will find her out and he'll run to me for sympathy. I'll not give it him. Not after this . . . Cheer up,' he said. 'The world is big. There's hope.'

'Of course.' But suddenly I saw the women's long, scowling faces over their lupins and their poppies, and my room in Torrington Square and the iron bars of my bedstead, and I thought, 'Not for me.'

'It may all be necessary,' he said, as if he were talking to himself. 'One has to get an entirely different set of values to be any good.'

I said, 'Do you think I could go out through the window? I don't want to meet them.'

'I'll come to the car with you. What's this man like?'

'Well, he's a bit like the man this morning, and he says he doesn't care for the sound of you.'

'Then I think I won't come. Go through the window and I'll hand your suitcase to you.'

He leaned out and said, 'See you in September, Petronella. I'll be back in September.'

I looked up at him. 'All right. Same address.'

The farmer said, 'I was coming in after you. You're well rid of that lot – never did like that sort. Too many of them about.'

'They're all right.'

'Well, tune up,' he said, and I sang 'Mr Brown, Mr Brown, Had a violin, Went around, went around, With his violin.' I sang all the way to Cirencester.

At the station he gave me my ticket and a box of chocolates.

'I bought these for you this afternoon, but I forgot them. Better hurry – there's not much time.

'Fare you well,' he said. 'That's what they say in Norfolk, where I come from.'

'Goodbye.'

'No, say fare you well.'

'Fare you well.'

The train started.

'This is very nice,' I thought, 'my first-class carriage', and had a long look at myself in the glass for the first time since it had happened. 'Never mind,' I said, and remembered Marston saying 'Never mind, never mind.'

'Don't look so down in the mouth, my girl,' I said to myself. '*Look gay.*'

35

'Cheer up,' I said, and kissed myself in the cool glass. I stood with my forehead against it and watched my face clouding gradually, then turned because I felt as if someone was staring at me, but it was only the girl on the cover of the chocolate-box. She had slanting green eyes, but they were too close together, and she had a white, square, smug face that didn't go with the slanting eyes. 'I bet you could be a rotten, respectable, sneering bitch too, with a face like that, if you had a chance,' I told her.

The train got into Paddington just before ten. As soon as I was on the platform I remembered the chocolates, but I didn't go back for them. 'Somebody will find you, somebody will look after you, you rotten, sneering, stupid, tight-mouthed bitch,' I thought.

London always smells the same. 'Frowsty,' you think, 'but I'm glad to be back.' And just for a while it bears you up. 'Anything's round the corner,' you think. But long before you get round the corner it lets you drop.

I decided that I'd walk for a bit with the suitcase and get tired and then perhaps I'd sleep. But at the corner of Marylebone Road and Edgware Road my arm was stiff and I put down the suitcase and waved at a taxi standing by the kerb.

'Sorry, miss,' the driver said, 'this gentleman was first.'

The young man smiled. 'It's all right. You have it.'

'You have it,' he said. The other one said, 'Want a lift?'

'I can get the next one. I'm not in any hurry.'

'Nor am I.'

The taxi driver moved impatiently.

'Well, don't let's hesitate any longer,' the young man said, 'or we'll lose our taximeter-cab. Get in – I can easily drop you wherever you're going.'

'Go along Edgware Road,' he said to the driver. 'I'll tell you where in a minute.'

The taxi started.

'Where to?'

'Torrington Square.'

The house would be waiting for me. 'When I pass Estelle's door,' I thought, 'there'll be no smell of scent now.' Then I was back in my small room on the top floor, listening to the church clock chiming every quarter-hour. 'There's a good time coming for the ladies. There's a good time coming for the girls . . .'

I said, 'Wait a minute. I don't want to go to Torrington Square.'

'Oh, you don't want to go to Torrington Square?' He seemed amused and wary, but more wary than amused.

'It's such a lovely night, so warm. I don't want to go home just yet. I think I'll go and sit in Hyde Park.'

'Not Torrington Square,' he shouted through the window.

The taxi drew up.

'Damn his eyes, what's he done that for?'

The driver got down and opened the door.

'Here, where am I going to? This is the third time you've changed your mind since you 'ailed me.'

'You'll go where you're damn well told.'

'Well where am I damn well told?'

'Go to Marble Arch.'

''Yde Park,' the driver said, looking us up and down and grinning broadly. Then he got back into his seat.

'I can't bear some of these chaps, can you?' the young man said.

When the taxi stopped at the end of Park Lane we both got out without a word. The driver looked us up and down again scornfully before he started away.

'What do you want to do in Hyde Park? Look at the trees?'

He took my suitcase and walked along by my side.

'Yes, I want to look at the trees and not go back to the place where I live. Never go back.'

'I've never lived in a place I like,' I thought, 'never.'

'That does sound desperate. Well, let's see if we can find a secluded spot.'

'That chair over there will do,' I said. It was away from people under a tree. Not that people mattered much, for now it was night and they are never so frightening then.

I shut my eyes so that I could hear and smell the trees better. I imagined I could smell water too. The Serpentine – I didn't know we had walked so far.

He said, 'I can't leave you so disconsolate on this lovely night – this night of love and night of stars.' He gave a loud hiccup, and then another. 'That always happens when I've eaten quails.'

'It happens to me when I'm tight.'

'Does it?' He pulled another chair forward and sat down by

my side. 'I can't leave you now until I know where you're going with that large suitcase and that desperate expression.'

I told him that I had just come back after a stay in the country, and he told me that he did not live in London, that his name was Melville and that he was at a loose end that evening.

'Did somebody let you down?'

'Oh, that's not important – not half so important as the desperate expression. I noticed that as soon as I saw you.'

'That's not despair, it's hunger,' I said, dropping into the backchat. 'Don't you know hunger when you see it?'

'Well, let's go and have something to eat, then. But where?' He looked at me uncertainly. 'Where?'

'We could go to the Apple Tree. Of course, it's a bit early, but we might be able to get kippers or eggs and bacon or sausages and mash.'

'The Apple Tree? I've heard of it. Could we go there?' he said, still eyeing me.

'We could indeed. You could come as my guest. I'm a member. I was one of the first members,' I boasted.

I had touched the right spring – even the feeling of his hand on my arm changed. *Always the same spring to touch before the sneering expression will go out of their eyes and the sneering sound out of their voices. Think about it – it's very important.*

'Lots of pretty girls at the Apple Tree, aren't there?' he said.

'I can't promise anything. It's a bad time of year for the Apple Tree, the singing and the gold.'

'Now what are you talking about?'

'Somebody I know calls it that.'

'But you'll be there.' He pulled his chair closer and looked round cautiously before he kissed me. 'And you're an awfully pretty girl, aren't you? . . . The Apple Tree, the singing and the gold. I like that.'

'Better than "Night of love and night of stars"?'

'Oh, they're not in the same street.'

I thought, 'How do you know what's in what street? How do they know who's fifth-rate, who's fifth-rate and where the devouring spider lives?'

'You don't really mind where we go, do you?' he said.

'I don't mind at all.'

He took his arm away. 'It was odd our meeting like that, wasn't it?'

'I don't think so. I don't think it was odd at all.'

After a silence, 'I haven't been very swift in the uptake, have I?' he said.

'No, you haven't. Now, let's be off to the Apple Tree, the singing and the gold.'

'Oh, damn the Apple Tree. I know a better place than that.'

'I've been persuaded to taste it before,' Marston said. *'It tasted exactly as I thought it would.'*

And everything was exactly as I had expected. The knowing waiters, the touch of the ice-cold wine glass, the red plush chairs, the food you don't notice, the gold-framed mirror, the bed in the room beyond that always looks as if its ostentatious whiteness hides dinginess.

But Marston should have said, 'It tastes of nothing, my dear, it tastes of nothing . . .'

When we got out into Leicester Square again I had forgotten Marston and only thought about how, when we had nothing better to do, Estelle and I would go to the Corner House or to some cheap restaurant in Soho and have dinner. She was so earnest when it came to food. 'You must have one good meal a day,' she would say, 'it is *necessary*.' *Escalope de veau* and fried potatoes and brussels sprouts, we usually had, and then *crème caramel* or *compôte de fruits*. And she seemed to be walking along by my side, wearing her blue suit and her white blouse, her high heels tapping. But as we turned the corner by the Hippodrome she vanished. I thought, 'I shall never see her again – I know it.'

In the taxi he said, 'I don't forget addresses, do I?'

'No, you don't.'

To keep myself awake I began to sing 'Mr Brown, Mr Brown, Had a violin . . .'

'Are you on the stage?'

'I was. I started my brilliant and successful career like so many others, in the chorus. But I wasn't a success.'

'What a shame! Why?'

'Because I couldn't say "epigrammatic".'

He laughed – really laughed that time.

'The stage manager had the dotty idea of pulling me out of my obscurity and giving me a line to say. The line was "Oh, Lottie, Lottie, don't be epigrammatic". I rehearsed it and rehearsed it, but when it came to the night it was just a blank.'

At the top of Charing Cross Road the taxi was held up. We were both laughing so much that people turned round and stared at us.

'It was one of the most dreadful moments of my life, and I shan't ever forget it. There was the stage manager, mouthing at me from the wings – he was the prompter too and he also played a small part, the family lawyer – and there he was all dressed up in grey-striped trousers and a black tailcoat and top hat and silver side-whiskers, and there I was, in a yellow dress and a large straw hat and a green sunshade and a lovely background of an English castle and garden – half ruined and half not, you know – and a chorus of footmen and maids, and my mind a complete blank.'

The taxi started again. 'Well, what happened?'

'Nothing. After one second the other actors went smoothly on. I remember the next line. It was "Going to Ascot? Well, if you don't get into the Royal Enclosure when you *are* there I'm no judge of character." '

'But what about the audience?'

'Oh, the audience weren't surprised because, you see, they had never expected me to speak at all. Well, here we are.'

I gave him my latchkey and he opened the door.

'A formidable key! It's like the key of a prison,' he said.

Everyone had gone to bed and there wasn't even a ghost of Estelle's scent in the hall.

'We must see each other again,' he said. 'Please. Couldn't you write to me at –' He stopped. 'No, I'll write to you. If you're ever – I'll write to you anyway.'

I said, 'Do you know what I want? I want a gold bracelet with blue stones in it. Not too blue – the darker blue I prefer.'

'Oh, well.' He was wary again. 'I'll do my best, but I'm not one of these plutocrats, you know.'

'Don't you dare to come back without it. But I'm going away for a few weeks. I'll be here again in September.'

'All right, I'll see you in September, Petronella,' he said chirpily, anxious to be off. 'And you've been so sweet to me.'

'The pleasure was all mine.'

He shook his head. 'Now, Lottie, Lottie, don't be epigrammatic.'

I thought, 'I daresay he would be nice if one got to know him. I daresay, perhaps . . .' listening to him tapping goodbye on the other side of the door. I tapped back twice and then started up the stairs. Past the door of Estelle's room, not feeling a thing as I passed it, because she had gone and I knew she would not ever come back.

In my room I stood looking out of the window, remembering my yellow dress, the blurred mass of the audience and the face of one man in the front row seen quite clearly, and how I thought, as quick as lightning, 'Help me, tell me what I have forgotten.' But though he had looked, as it seemed, straight into my eyes, and though I was sure he knew exactly what I was thinking, he had not helped me. He had only smiled. He had left me in that moment that seemed like years standing there until through the dreadful blankness of my mind I had heard a high, shrill, cockney voice saying, 'Going to Ascot?' and seen the stage manager frown and shake his head at me.

43

'My God, I must have looked a fool,' I thought, laughing and feeling the tears running down my face.

'What a waste of good tears!' the other girls had told me when I cried in the dressing-room that night. 'Oh, the waste, the waste, the waste!'

But that did not last long.

'What's the time?' I thought, and because I wasn't sleepy any longer I sat down in the chair by the window, waiting for the clock outside to strike.

Rapunzel, Rapunzel

During the three weeks I had been in the hospital I would often see a phantom village when I looked out of the window instead of the London plane trees. It was an Arab village or my idea of one, small white houses clustered together on a hill. This hallucination would appear and disappear and I'd watch for it, feeling lost when a day passed without my seeing it.

One morning I was told that I must get ready to leave as I was now well enough for a short stay in a convalescent home. I had to dress and get packed very quickly and what between my haste and unsteady legs I got into the car waiting outside the hospital without any idea of where it was going to take me.

We drove for about forty minutes, stopping twice to pick up other patients. We were still in London but what part of London? Norwood perhaps? Richmond? Beckenham?

The convalescent home, when we reached it, was an imposing red brick building with a fairly large garden. The other patients went into a room on the ground floor and I walked up the staircase by myself, clutching the banisters. At the top a pretty but unsmiling Indian nurse greeted me, showed me into a ward, helped me unpack and saw me into bed. There was a lot of talking and laughing going on and a radio was playing; it was confusing after the comparative quiet of the hospital. I shut my eyes and when I opened them a young good-looking doctor was standing near me. He asked a few questions and finally where my home was.

'I live in Devon now.'

'And have you been to any hunt balls lately?'

This was so unexpected that it was a second or two before I managed to smile and say that they must be great fun but that I'd never been to a hunt ball and didn't know what they were like. He lost interest and went over to the next bed.

I couldn't sleep for a long time, the radio and the conversation went on interminably and I was relieved when, early next morning, a nurse told me that I was to be moved into another room.

The new ward was smaller and quieter. There were about fourteen patients but I was still too weary to notice anybody except my immediate neighbour, an elderly woman with piles of glossy magazines at the foot of her bed. She pored over them and played her radio all day. That night we had an argument, she said I ought to put my light out and not keep everybody awake because I wanted to read, I said that it wasn't yet ten o'clock and that her radio had annoyed me all day, but I soon gave in. Perhaps I was keeping the others awake.

Somebody was snoring; just as I thought the noise had stopped it would start up louder than ever and though I had asked for a sleeping pill, it seemed hours before it worked and when I did eventually sleep I had a long disturbing dream which I couldn't remember when I woke up. I only knew that I was extremely glad to be awake.

When I looked at my neighbour her slim back was turned towards me and she was brushing her hair – there was a great deal of it – long, silvery white, silky. She brushed away steadily, rhythmically, for some time. She must have taken great care of it all her life and now there it all was, intact, to comfort and reassure her that she was still herself. Even when she had pinned it up into a loose bun it fell so prettily round her face that it was difficult to think of her as an old lady.

I can't say that we ever became friendly. She told me that she was an Australian, that her name was Peterson, and once she lent me a glossy magazine.

I hadn't been there long when I realized that I didn't like the convalescent home and that the sooner I got out of it the better I'd be pleased. The monotony of the hospital had finally had a soothing effect. I'd felt weak, out of love with life, but resigned and passive; here on the contrary I was anxious, restless and yet it ought to have been a comforting place. The passage outside the ward was carpeted in dark red, dark red curtains hung over the tall window at the far end and the staircase had a spacious look, with its wide shallow steps and broad oak banisters – just the sort of house to get well in, you would have thought. But I felt it shut in, brooding, even threatening in its stolid way.

The matron soon insisted on my taking daily exercise in the garden and another patient usually walked at the same time as I did. She always carried a paper bag of boiled sweets which she'd offer to me as we discussed her operation for gall bladder and my heart attack in detail. But all the time I was thinking that there too the trees drooped in a heavy, melancholy way and the grass was a much darker colour than ordinary grass. Something about the whole place reminded me of a placid citizen, respectable and respected, who would poison anyone disliked or disapproved of at the drop of a hat.

No kind ladies came round with trolleys of books, as they had in the hospital, so one day I asked if it wasn't possible for me to have something to read. I was told that there was a library on the ground floor, 'Down the stairs,' said the nurse, 'and to your left.'

When I went in the blinds were drawn and I was in semi-darkness but I was so certain that I wasn't alone that I stopped near the door and felt for the light switch. The room was empty except for a large table in the middle with straight-backed chairs arranged round it, as if for a meal, and a rickety bookcase at the far end. There was no one there. No one! 'Oh don't be idiotic,' I said aloud and walked past the table. The books leant up against each other disconsolately. They had a forlorn, neglected appearance as though no one had looked at or touched them for years. They would have been less reproachful piled in a heap to be thrown away. Most of them were memoirs or African adventures by early Victorian travellers, in very close print. I didn't look long, for I hated turning my back on that table, those chairs and when I saw a torn Tauchnitz paperback by a writer I'd heard of I grabbed it and hurried out as quickly as I could. Nothing would have induced me to go back to that room and I read and reread the book steadily, never taking in what I was reading, so that now I can't remember the title or what it was about. It was after this that I began counting: 'Only eight days more, only six days more.'

One morning a trim little man looked into the ward and asked 'Does any lady want a shampoo or haircut?'

Silence except for a few firm 'No thank yous'.

Then Mrs Peterson said: 'Yes, I should like my hair trimmed, please, if it could be managed.'

'Okay,' said the man, 'tomorrow morning at eleven.'

When he had gone someone said: 'He's a man's barber, you know.'

'I just want it trimmed. I have to be careful about split ends,' said the Australian.

Next morning the barber appeared with all his paraphernalia, put a chair near a basin – there was no looking glass above it – and smilingly invited her to sit down. She said something to him, he nodded and proceeded while everybody watched covertly. She sat up and he dried her hair gently. Then he picked it up in one hand and produced a large pair of scissors. Snip, snip, and half of it was lying on the floor. One woman gasped.

Mrs Peterson put her hand up uneasily and felt her neck but said nothing. She must have realized that something was wrong but couldn't know the extent of the damage of course, and it all happened very quickly. The rest went and in a few minutes she had disappeared under the dryer while the barber

49

tidied up. When she paid him he said: 'You'll be glad to be rid of the weight of it, won't you dear?' She didn't answer.

'Cheerio ladies.' He went off carrying the hair that he had so carefully collected in a plastic bag.

He hadn't made a very good job of setting what was left and her face looked large, naked and rather plain. She still seemed utterly astonished as she walked back to bed. Then she reached for her handglass and stared at herself for a long time. When I saw how distressed she grew as she looked I whispered: 'Don't worry, you'll be surprised how quickly it'll grow again.'

'No, there isn't time,' she said, turned, pulled the sheet up high and lay so still that I thought she was asleep, but I heard her say, not to me or anybody else, 'Nobody will want me now.'

During the night I was woken to hear her being violently sick. A nurse hurried to her bed. Next morning it started again, she apologized feebly to the matron who came along to look at her. 'I'm so very sorry to trouble you, I'm so very sorry.'

All day at intervals it went on, the vomiting, the chokings, the weak child's voice saying: 'I'm so sorry, I'm so sorry', and by night they had a screen up round her bed.

I stopped listening to the sounds coming from behind the screen, for one gets used to anything. But when, one morning, I saw that it had been taken away and that the bed was empty and tidy I was annoyed to hear a woman say: 'They always take them away like that. Quietly. In the night.'

'These people are so damned gloomy,' I said to myself.

'She'll probably get perfectly well, her hair will grow again and soon look very pretty.'

I'd be leaving the convalescent home the day after tomorrow. Why wasn't I thinking of that instead of a story read long ago in the Blue or Yellow fairy book (perhaps the Crimson) and the words repeating themselves so unreasonably in my head: 'Rapunzel, Rapunzel, let down your hair'?

I Used to Live Here Once

She was standing by the river looking at the stepping stones and remembering each one. There was the round unsteady stone, the pointed one, the flat one in the middle – the safe stone where you could stand and look round. The next wasn't so safe, for when the river was full the water flowed over it and even when it showed dry it was slippery. But after that it was easy and soon she was standing on the other side.

The road was much wider than it used to be but the work had been done carelessly. The felled trees had not been cleared away and the bushes looked trampled. Yet it was the same road and she walked along feeling extraordinarily happy.

It was a fine day, a blue day. The only thing was that the sky had a glassy look that she didn't remember. That was the only word she could think of. Glassy. She turned the corner, saw that what had been the old *pavé* had been taken up, and there too the road was much wider, but it had the same unfinished look.

She came to the worn stone steps that led up to the house and her heart began to beat. The screw pine was gone, so was the mock summer house called the *ajoupa*, but the clove tree was still there and at the top of the steps the rough lawn stretched away, just as she remembered it. She stopped and looked towards the house that had been added to and painted white. It was strange to see a car standing in front of it.

There were two children under the big mango tree, a boy and a little girl, and she waved to them and called 'Hello' but they didn't answer her or turn their heads. Very fair children, as Europeans born in the West Indies so often are: as if the white blood is asserting itself against all odds.

The grass was yellow in the hot sunlight as she walked towards them. When she was quite close she called again shyly: 'Hello.' Then, 'I used to live here once,' she said.

Still they didn't answer. When she said for the third time 'Hello' she was quite near them. Her arms went out instinctively with the longing to touch them.

It was the boy who turned. His grey eyes looked straight into hers. His expression didn't change. He said: 'Hasn't it gone cold all of a sudden. D'you notice? Let's go in.' 'Yes let's,' said the girl.

Her arms fell to her sides as she watched them running across the grass to the house. That was the first time she knew.